Being Serviced

D1810383

This is a work of fiction. Any resemblance of characters to actual

Persons, living or dead are purely coincidental. The Author holds exclusive rights to

this work. Unauthorized duplication is prohibited.

This material is intended for mature audiences only

Warning: this story contains graphic descriptions of sexual content including adultery, interracial lust, and cuckold fantasies.

Getting prepped for the trip

It was finally Saturday morning. Trisha and Mike had been looking forward to this day for at least three weeks. Tonight was party night and the couple had already packed bags for the trip down to Charlotte the night before.

As always, Mike was able to get everything into the size of a gym bag, needing a larger bag only to store the jug of Irish Crème liqueur that was his favorite sipping brew at parties such as this. Of course, he had his fifth of rum for later in the evening once the party really got underway and as offerings to guys who would visit their room that evening. Mostly, the rum was there to keep people out of his Irish Crème.

He also included a small bottle of Southern Comfort for Trish. Although neither Trisha nor Mike drank that often, play parties such as tonights have never seemed complete without some alcohol. The Southern Comfort would also limit the amount of Mike's prized elixir that Trisha would consume. Moreover, the Southern Comfort would jump start dropping those initial inhibitions that Trisha always seemed to have at the beginning of these kinds of parties.

Trisha had finally given up on packing her bag. Bags actually, two full-sized suitcases just so she could have plenty of options for the evening. Different looks she could render to the men that awaited her. Mike finally stepped in and had her spread both bags open so he could help Trisha make her mind up about what to take.

He made sure that some of his favorite attire for her was there. Trisha had a white swimsuit top with something akin to black zebra stripes that when worn with just thigh highs and heals, was really hot looking. The top looked more like a mini-dress and had a dressed-up look to it that made Trisha standout in the common area where the men could socialize with the ladies who were there to be serviced that night. It made it much easier for Mike to keep an eye on what she was up to from a distance.

He also made sure that the near transparent black body stocking was included. He preferred that Trisha start the evening in the white swim top and then only later, after her first fuck, did he like seeing her in that body stocking. It had an open crotch area, which allowed her to take on number two without changing anything about her appearance. Occasionally, her partner would make that choice for her and remove it to get more direct skin on skin contact with her.

Later in the evening, it really did not matter much to Mike about what Trisha was wearing. The last party they had attended, which was about three months before. The same dude that was hosting tonight's party had hosted it. That last party, Trisha had walked out of their hotel room and down to the snack table completely naked. Mike had stood outside their room and watched as guys that were hanging out alongside the hallway walls tried to appear as if they weren't noticing. Of course, as she passed and proceeded down the hall, they were all eyes. Trisha knew that of course, her exhibitionist side was having the time of its life.

This party, like most of the ones that Mike and Trisha attended was focused on black men on white ladies. White couples would attend for the express purpose of making the wife available to the black singles. Occasionally, a white husband might approach one of the wives but usually, their advances brushed aside. These women were there for interracial.

A couple of years before, Mike and Trisha was at another BBC party when one of the wives approached Trisha and asked her if she would mind doing her husband. She told Trisha that her husband had not been laid in six months. The request touched Trisha and she said, "Sure, I'd be happy to." to the woman. While she was lending a hand, helping the poor man out, she was horrified to learn that not only had he not been laid for six months, his wife had not submitted to him for over two years. "That's fucked up!" she told Mike later that night.

Tonight's party was one of those full floor takeover events. There were about 25 individual rooms, mostly occupied by the white couples. Most of the men attending did not have their own room. Three suites would be available for public play. However, typically Trisha preferred that the door to our room be propped open so anytime she was in the room, it was a public play area also. She liked allowing other party guest to just walk in and watch her screwing and sucking dicks. All she required was that they do so quietly.

There had been one time when Trisha's open door policy nearly backfired. She had been flirting with two dudes in the social area, doing lap dances on them both and as she rubbed against them and teased them, she was definitely getting herself really turned on as well. When the moment finally came to head down to our room, she walked them both hand in hand down the hallway and I unlocked the door to let the three of them in. I left the door completely ajar as usual.

Trisha was kissing and touching and being enjoyed when a third dude stepped inside the room and instead of just watching, he joined the mix. Soon, the three men had Trisha completely naked and her mouth was moving from one big black cock to the next while her tits got fondled and sucked and she got fingered by them all. At one point, one of the three decided he was not ready to play and zipped his jeans up and left the room. Maybe he felt the size of his dick was not competitive enough with the other guys.

A few moments later, another dude caught a glimpse of the action taking place and he had no concerns about whether his dick was big enough. Trish never even noticed that there had been any changes in the lineup. Even if she had noticed, it would not have mattered to her. This was why she came to these parties.

At least two of the three men penetrated Trisha's pussy over the next twenty minutes or so and all of them spent time within Trisha's other opening. Trisha was not a three-hole slut like some of the other woman proudly proclaimed; her ass was off-limits to everyone and everything.

It was during all of this that a moment came when Trisha opened her eyes and glanced around the room. At least ten other men had entered the room, all hovering nearby watching the action. Each one looking for an access point to her, which with three men already engaged, was pretty hard to come by.

Mike had become a little concerned himself about all the dudes who had come into the room, as he set in the room's only chair, watching the action as it unfolded. He realized that there was a possibility that this could get out of hand and instead of it being a just a fun fuck party, it could turn into a gang rape. It was only his knowledge about how men reacted to a woman in distress that kept him from stepping up and shutting things down.

Mike knew that if any of the guys got squirrelly, and started doing things that Trisha didn't want him to, that virtually every other guy in the room would go ballistic on him for fucking up a good thing. Chivalry is not dead in situations like this, but not for the reasons portrayed in fairy tales... these people did not want some jerk messing with their food and they would turn on someone making waves like a pack of wolves. Therefore, Mike allowed the action to continue but he was on alert.

Mike felt intense excitement about having additional people in the room. He listened intently to what people were saying as the watched the live show. He especially enjoyed it when he overheard comments between the men such as "That white bitch is into it Bro."

As the play continued, one of the current participants got his nut off inside Trisha and backed away from things. That allowed another man to move into the space now left open. Trisha noticed the substitution this time and although she was not in the least bothered by having someone replaced, she did open her eyes just to see what this new person looked like that had just started feeling her up. This was when she also looked around the room and saw what was going on.

Seeing at least a dozen black men's faces surrounding her, she freaked out, but managed to shut things down really well. She just told everyone that she needed a little time to take a break and catch her breath and no one objected. Mike did raise his concerns a little when she did this, after all, most of the guys hadn't even had a chance to touch her yet.

Mike was secretly hoping that Trish would end up getting at least some dick from everyone in the room. Pulling a train was something that despite all the parties they had attended, was a description that he never felt was applicable.

There are rules enforced at these parties. Of course, the one rule that outshines all others is that "No means No." Another rule, which unfortunately tends to work against Trish's preferred way to behave as far as Mike was concerned, was that it was supposed to be Lady's Choice.

A number of the men who attended these parties felt it was their role to simply be there and allow the women to approach them if they were interested. Otherwise, leave the ladies alone. Trisha liked being seduced and Mike enjoyed seeing a man trying to seduce his wife more than he liked seeing them on top of her a bit later.

Mike liked the hunt himself, which was why he enjoyed seeing someone trying to get some off Trish. He could tell almost instantly whether Trisha was willing to fuck just by the way she moved, smiled, and leaned into someone who was hoping to score with her. Even at a party such as this where everyone knows why they are there, the guy never knows for sure until further into the conversation.

Mike would like it when a man moved in on her carefully at first, wading in to test the waters with Trish. Sometimes he would wince when he witnessed someone being too cautious because unless Trish was really rolling, she was unlikely to suggest "Wanna go play?" on her own.

Enroute

Finally, Mike was able to slim down Trisha's wardrobe enough to fit into her two suitcases. He could manage lugging them both from the car in one trip when they got to the hotel as long as Trisha was willing to handle Mike's small bag. For some reason, Mike never remembered that invariably, there would be at least one additional stop because Trisha would want to pick up some chips and other snack food, along with a couple of bottles of soda pop. He grimaced when, just as they were about to get into the car and head north to Charlotte, she reminded him to put the ice chest in the truck.

Although the party would have a snack table setup with finger sandwiches, chips and dip, and cookies galore, they both liked having their own small buffet setting in the room for both before the party got started as well as being a time saver later on when things were happening.

Miraculously, Mike and Trisha managed to pull out of the driveway by 10:30 am, only an hour later than what they had agreed should be the departure time. Parties like this, where it was a hundred miles away and included private rooms were treated somewhat like mini-vacations. There was more planned then just getting Trisha fucked a half dozen times.

There would arrive at the hotel and plead for access to their hotel suite even though check-in time was listed as 3pm. Usually, this was not a problem since the entire floor had been reserved for the party and the hotel often steered Friday night guest to other rooms if possible.

Mike never could figure out exactly what the hotel staff knew about what was going on. There would usually be a twenty-something female clerk at the front desk. Upon arrival, Mike would tell this innocent looking young lady their names and she would look them up on the reservations list. Did she know what people who were going to be staying on that floor were there for? How could they not?

The host of this particular party had his events every third Saturday of the month at this same hotel and had been throwing them for at least three years. Mike could not envision that staff gossip had not explored every detail of what went on at those parties.

This young smiling girl had probably long since stopped wondering why about 20 white couples were checking in and that as evening approached, about eighty young black studs hit the elevators to head to the reserved floor.

Finally on the road to Charlotte, Mike and Trisha kicked back a little as Mike allowed the cruise control to take over most of the driving chores. As usual, the plan was to hit Charlotte, check in, and haul all their junk up to the room. There would be a quick stop just before to pick up the snacks and Mike usually grabbed a couple of bags of ice for the cooler.

He thought it was unfair for him to expect that the hotel's ice machine should provide enough to fill an ice chest. Plus, a lot easier to carry up two ten pound ice bags then making a dozen trips back and forth using only one of those little in-room ice buckets.

Mike would usually fill up one of the small room glasses with ice and two-thirds full of Irish Crème to relax after his three trips to and from the car hauling all their stuff. He would set quietly, satisfied to be there after the drive, and watch Trisha as she busied herself with arranging her wardrobe into the closet and arranging the cabinet drawers so they were just right.

In addition to her two suitcases, Mike's overnight bag, the ice chest and bags of ice and all the chips and snack foods, there was also a large beach purse-like bag that contained all of their toiletries. There was Mike's tooth brush, tooth paste to be shared, a new razor, and the remaining ten pounds worth of lotions, makeup, manicure kits, etc that Trisha felt were absolutely necessary to have in the room.

Mike rarely drank and then drove which was one of the reasons he loved these overnight parties. But, the Irish Crème was so low in alcohol content that he knew one wouldn't matter. He finished his drink about the same time Trish finished arranging everything to her satisfaction. As planned, the next step was to go back out to the car and drive around the area, picking out a place to have lunch at some local restaurant that was not part of a chain.

They finally found what they were looking for. It was a chain restaurant but not one they visited around home. Lunch would be slow paced and relaxed. Talk of the night's party plans was rarely discussed. Too many big ears setting in adjoining booths.

Besides, Mike and Trish had already talked each other out about such topics of how many men she was going to fuck tonight on the drive down. Mike figured she would do at least three; Trisha was convinced that she should try for five. Her all time record was seven.

The plan had been to explore shopping opportunities and just sight see once lunch was over but neither of them was able to get much sleep the night before and the drive down plus the leisurely lunch had worn them down and they decided to just head back to the room to take a nap. After all, this was likely to be a late night before it was over.

They always made plans to do more than just eat and go back to the room and occasionally, they actually did manage a little wandering around through Charlotte. Often, they would end up at adult stores because Trisha was always on the lookout for special things to have just for the night's party.

Upon exiting the elevator on the party floor, they ran into their host William. He welcomed them and went on about his task of getting a registration table setup just outside the elevator. The security staff was helping him set things up. He came over and gave Trisha a hug and kiss, as he usually did and then went back about his business.

Mike knew that Trisha would love to fuck William sometime but it was his practice to abstain from playing at parties. He wanted to insure that the event ran smoothly and no one got overly intoxicated or caused any scenes.

However, William did one thing right that helped him continue to get white women to his parties. He always put up the pretense that if he had the time right now, nothing he would like better then to have a little pre-party fun with each of the ladies.

"Have fun tonight," he told them, as they headed down the hall to their room. "We will," they said without looking back.

Mike always requested a room with two double beds. This way, if Trish wanted to allow one of the guys to stay overnight with her, he wouldn't need to be in the bed with them and in their way. It would also allow him to pretend to sleep when the inevitable middle of the night action took place. Mike liked doing that, he felt that Trish was more likely to act he wasn't there.

Mike also amused himself by telling Trish to try to keep her action in her own bed that night so that Mike would not have to deal with wet slimy spots on the bed.

Mike closed off the window curtains and turned out the room lights and despite it being the middle of the afternoon, the room was pretty dark. Trisha somehow managed to fall asleep within minutes of lying on her bed while Mike just tossed and turned. He was way too excited about the events to come to sleep. About three hours passed before Mike gave up on sleeping.

The damn thing was, he was just now starting to feel sleepy but it was getting close to party time now. As he lay there in his bed, he occasionally heard voices out in the hallway. Usually, he heard women's voice speaking, other couples with their own rooms checking in for the evenings play.

Finally, at 6pm, Mike gave up trying. He thought that perhaps, there might have been two or three short catnaps of thirty minutes or less each. He stripped naked and headed for the shower where he shaved under the nozzle using the steam and wash soap to soften the small growth he had accumulated since Friday morning. When he came out, Trisha had also awakened. She was pulling bottles of lotion and some condoms out of her makeup bag and placing them strategically in the night stand drawer between the two beds. She also made sure her collection of vibrators and other toys was within easy reach.

She always intended to use protection at these parties but most of the time; she ended up tossing all of the condoms back into her bags the next morning. Of late, she had even begun to lose all pretenses about condom use and simply commented that they were there if anyone wanted to use them.

The plain truth was that Trisha loved how it felt when a man came deep inside her. She liked the warmth, and she even liked the idea of it dripping out and down her leg afterwards. There may have been some extra stimuli, based on pregnancy risk, but of course, this was not too likely since she was on birth control.

She was also aware that for some men, the act of putting on a condom tended to deflate their enthusiasm. She had even tried to learn the skill of applying a condom on a dick using her mouth but that still did not work in many cases.

Mike was always amused at this. He had not worn a condom himself since he was a teenager but what he remembered was that the feelings he had when he rolled it down over his dick had the opposite effect. It tended to make him hard even if he was somewhat flaccid when he started.

Mike was dressed and had fixed himself another Irish Crème when Trisha started up her bath water. A long, relaxing bubble bath was Trish's way of getting her mind wrapped around things she knew would come.

He watched TV, occasionally wandered around the hotel floor seeing who was there and chatting with the security guys. Several of the rooms had their doors open and occasionally he would catch glimpses of the people inside but he did not intrude. Usually, the occupants were just chilling out in front of the TV or arranging their stuff in the drawers and closets. The next two hours would really drag for him as he waited for the action to start.

Finally, Trisha emerged from the bathroom, wearing a towel wrapped around her middle and another one arranged turban style on her head. As she came into the room, she noticed that the door was wide open and she walked over and closed it casually. Mike knew that if they had been on a real vacation, staying at a hotel where normal stuff was happening, that she would have freaked a bit and told Mike in hushed tones to close the damn door. However, here, she was not too concerned. She just wanted to finish her preparations without being bothered by someone wanting to knock off a piece before the party started.

Mike was on his eighth stroll up and down the hallway when on the way back, he spotted Trisha wearing that white and black swim top heading his way. Her legs sheathed by dark toned panty hose. He liked the look but he was not a fan of panty hose. His preference was the thigh highs, held up simply because they were fresh out of the package and with Trisha wearing nothing else but the socks and the top.

Trisha went straight to the buffet table, which was totally stocked and ready to go, and foraged for a few items to put on her paper plate. After she had selected her appetizers, she walked over to where Mike was leaning and asked him "What's up?"

Party Time

The two of them small talked a bit and then wandered away from each other. Both of them felt that things went smoother if Trisha did not appear to be hard wired to Mike. It would help encourage the men that wanted to approach her if there was not a man standing next to her. That was not true of all the couples. Many times, they had seen couples arm and arm for the entire evening, even while one of the party guys was making a move on the wife.

It was still really early. There were maybe two other white couples and perhaps a half a dozen black men wandering the floor. There was even a solo white fellow hanging out. Mike did not rate the white dude's chances as being very good that night, and in fact, the man never did get to play with anyone.

These women were there for sex with black men, with their husband's permission and often with their husbands viewing the activity. These women liked being described as Black Cock Whores.

Some of the couples preferred threesomes, for others like Mike and Trisha, the husband preferred the role of voyeur although after having seen Trisha being black fucked possibly five hundred times, it was not necessary for him to watch. It would be a scene so familiar, that it was tantamount to watching Star Wars again.

Nearly another hour passed. Occasionally they would meet somewhere in the middle and chitchat a few minutes and then both would take up new positions within the party common areas. Mike always made sure he could see Trish most of the time. She tended to focus more on the other people wandering around, knowing that Mike was always lurking somewhere close by.

Typically, even with an eight o'clock scheduled start, things did not really get going until at least nine and sometimes even 10 o'clock. Mike went back to their hotel room to fix his forth

Irish Crème on the rocks, this time with a shot of rum to spice it up a little. When he emerged, he spotted Trish standing close to someone who must have been a tad over six foot and the two of them were chatting intently, whispering actually. Mike knew Trish's body language well enough to know she intended to fuck this man. He also had no doubts that the man was very interested in being fucked by Trish.

Mike just walked by his wife and the stranger without appearing to pay any attention but he did not stray too far off this time. A few moments later, he saw Trisha look in his direction and she motioned him to join them.

Trisha started with "Tony, this is my husband Mike." The two men eyed each other for a second and then quickly extended their arms to shake hands. Speaking to Mike, Trisha declared, "Tony is going to give me a massage." The big smile from Tony confirmed that this was his desire too.

"Cool" was all Mike said and the three of them walked towards Mike and Trisha's hotel room. Mike unlocked it but left the door open as usual. Tony looked a little on edge but got over it really quick as Trisha flung the swim top over her head and over onto the other bed. She then reached into the nightstand, pulled out one of her bottles of lotion, and handed it to Tony. She flopped down belly first onto the bed and waited for him to get things started.

Tony squeezed out a goodly glob of the stuff onto one hand and then used both hands to warm it up before touching Trisha. He started with her back and shoulders, worked his way over her buttocks and up and down her legs. Trisha cooed occasionally, offered an occasional suggestion about what part of her should be attended to next.

Mike knew his wife really well. He knew that for Trisha, this was one of the high points of the night. She loved being massaged. Occasionally Mike would tell Trisha that she was a massage whore... and, for some reason this amused Trisha rather than angered her.

This was a fuck party. Trisha had come to get fucked and fucked a lot. However, massage... this was her foreplay and she would not be happy with anyone's dick until she had her body properly prepared. She was definitely getting into being massaged by Tony. He was not too rough, not too light, he was just right, as Goldilocks would say.

After a while, Tony added a few short kisses to her shoulders and around her neck, nibbling an ear lobe while he was there and Trisha's giggles told him he was doing what she wanted him to.

Tony applied his fourth handful of lotion but this time he only rubbed in it enough to get it spread out and he started pulling off his jeans. Mike could see that he was already semi-erect. Mike guessed he was just short of eight inches but longer than thick. That was good because he knew Trisha liked to be warmed up thoroughly down there before someone tried sticking a dick about the size of a coke can into her.

Tony tossed off his shirt also but left on his socks. Mike frowned a little at that, neither he nor Trisha thought it was good manners to leave your fucking socks on. However, not a big deal. It just seemed odd to them. Almost like the man was worried about things and wanted to at least have socks on his feet in case he needed to make a quick getaway.

Tony slide in beside Trisha and she edged over to her right so that he had room to get his full body on the bed with her. He continued to massage her but now he was also kissing her lips and he turned her so that they were face to face. He focused his massage on Trisha's nipples and even though the light was subdued within the room, Mike could see that her tits were pushed out and firm.

"This is going well," thought Mike.

It wasn't long before Tony had explored most of Trisha's body with his hands and his mouth. He didn't go down on her but he did spend quite a bit of time playing with the outside and top of Trisha's vagina. Mike, settled back now trying to avoid making any sounds or movements that might interfere, he knew that Tony was doing a great job and that this was just the way his wife liked that first encounter to be.

"Yes, going to be a great night," Mike thought to himself. He wanted a refill on his Irish Crème but knew the timing wasn't right. He would wait until Tony was fucking the shit out of her before he would get up and rattle ice cubes into his glass.

About then, he saw that Trish was going to go on the offensive and she set up and said, "Now, let me do you a little." She reached towards the lotion that had been placed on top the nightstand. She only gave Tony about five minutes worth of massage before diving down on his dick and sucking on it and licking all sides of it. She was kissing it now also, along with the licks. She loved making love to a dick. Worshiping it.

Trisha really enjoyed the feel of a penis in her hand. She often told Mike that one of her favorite things was to go down on a man that was not totally erect and feel it harden up and lengthen in her hand and mouth. Of course, it was black dick that most satisfied her desires. Not long after Trisha started going down on him, Tony felt that he needed to be inside so he rose up and gently laid her down and climbed on top of her.

At first, Trisha engulfed him with her legs but Tony apparently felt this was too confining on him. He wanted to pull out as far as he could and then plunge himself down as deep as he could into her. He reached around and grabbed both of Trisha's ankles and lifted her legs up so that they rested on his shoulders.

Trisha did not ask him whether he wanted to use a condom. Mike was not a bit surprised. He knew what she preferred.

Sometimes at these things, she would start out using one, maybe even using one on her second of the night. Trish's routines were well known to Mike. After she finished taking on Tony, she would go into the bathroom and wash him out of her using one of the half dozen plastic douche bottles she had brought. However, before the night was over, neither she nor any of the guys still at it would give a shit about whether Trish's pussy was squeezing some other guy's cum out with every stroke.

After a while, Tony flipped her over and pulled her towards the edge of the bed. He got to his feet, pulled her butt towards his cock, and finished up in her doggy style. By then Mike was ready for another refill on his Irish Crème. The bottle was still half-full, but it was a very large bottle. Mike felt a slight buzz but figured that he was about where he wanted to be at that point in the evening.

Afterwards, we all set around for a bit. Trish was asked if it would be possible for Tony to call her occasionally, to hook up and hang out now and then and Trish reached into the nightstand and yanked a page out of a small spiral notebook and gave it to him after jotting down her phone number.

Mike guessed that there was well over a hundred black dudes within two hours drive of where they lived that had Trisha's phone number, and a lot of them had fucked her at least once. She got a lot of phone calls but no where nearly as many as Mike would have thought considering how wide spread her contact information had become over the last four or five years.

Occasionally, one of her guy friends would call and come over and fuck her. What she liked was when they wanted more than just a fuck. She liked it when they asked her out. Over time, those that did offer her more than just a dick found her far more willing to say yes than those that did not. It was not about them spending money for dinner or something like that... a date to go window-shopping was better than just booty-calls.

Tony was local to the Charlotte area however, so both Trisha and Mike felt it was more of a courtesy request for the number than any serious interest in future events. Regardless, he had been exactly what she had come for and a perfect start for the evening so, if he did call and not too many moons had passed since he had been with her, Mike was sure she would be very willing to accommodate his needs again.

As expected, once Tony had left the room, Trisha closed the open room door and secluded herself into the bathroom to prepare herself for the next guy. This would be the only time all night when the room door would be shut unless neither of us were inside the room. She felt douching was a private thing. Mike didn't care to watch that stuff either. In fact, he refreshed his drink, adding a bit of rum for taste, and went out to see how the crowd looked now that it was getting later in the evening.

It was just after 10pm. By now, there looked to be several dozen people scattered around in the hallways and in the open party suites. He noticed that no one was actually playing in the group suites but there were many people inside the rooms, setting on chairs and leaning against walls as if they were waiting for the show to start.

About fifteen minutes later, Mike caught sight of Trisha heading in his direction. She had obviously retouched her makeup. Tony had managed to lick and smear her carefully applied facial enhancements during their play. She had re-donned the white swim top but this time Mike saw that she was barelegged and barefooted. He doubted if she had bothered putting panties on either.

Seeing her bare feet, he knew that this alone would get a few eyes following her. When Trish and he had first jumped into the whole Swingers Lifestyle thing, he had been surprised at just how many people were into feet.

He was waiting to ask her "Well, how did you like Tony?" but she just walked past him as if he was not there. Of course, she saw him, but she figured that Mike had no great need for hearing about what had just happened. He was right there watching and listening to it all. Frankly Mike didn't give a shit either… he was much more interested to see who would fuck her next. Time enough for a recap on the drive home tomorrow.

Over the next twenty minutes or so, the two of them would migrate between strategic positions at various points around the public areas but no one else had approached her yet. Mike felt that his buzz had dissipated and that he needed to fuel up a bit. This was a major reason he liked hitting the ABC store and picking up those oversized bottles of Irish Crème. He could sip his drinks all night long and not get drunk. He also liked the fact that he usually avoided a hangover the next day. Of course, that would depend upon how much of the rum he used during the course of the night.

He used the party's ice chest to fill one of the red plastic cups. His own ice storage was getting a bit watery. These cups would hold about three times the content that those little in-room glasses held and he headed towards the room to fill it up. He spent about five minutes there, taking time to urinate. He flipped on the TV just to see if the room had access to HBO and then flipped it back off and headed back towards the snacks table area.

He looked around but Trish was nowhere to be found. He made a quick circle up and down both hallway isles, looped through the open playroom areas, but he did not spot her. He figured that she was probably behind one of the closed room doors, being fucked again of course.

He made another loop through the hallways looking inside each room briefly when the door was open. Many were but he only caught sight of one woman being fucked. She was white of course, and the two fellows on her were both black but it was not Trisha.

Convinced now that Trish was off doing a thing with someone, Mike went back to their room and flipped on the TV again but he couldn't get interested in anything. He had no problems with Trish being fucked somewhere without him there, and often when the couple entertained at home, Trish would make it a solo while Mike listened to the sounds of the bed banging against the wall upstairs. However, at parties, he felt it was more fun to participate, by being there to watch.

After a while, Mike went back out into the crowd and then wandered into one of the open party rooms and set down. There was a guy setting nearby and the two of them started chatting. The stranger's name was Jamal and apparently had driven in to Charlotte from Columbia SC for the party.

Mike thought for a moment that it was too bad that he would have such a long drive home after the party. He entertained the idea of mentioning him to Trish once she re-emerged, suggest that maybe they could offer him some hospitality in Trish's bed overnight.

It was the idea of Jamal being an overnight guest for Trish that prompted Mike to engage the man in conversation about Trish. No promises were made and Mike never got into to talking about where Jamal was going to sleep that night. He knew Trish would probably have no problems with the idea but he knew he should at least ask her before he said anything to Jamal about the idea.

Mike and Jamal continued chatting for another twenty minutes or so. Neither of them sensed any need to be anywhere else. Of course, the subject of Trish was brought up. Mike did not get into any details. Considering where they were, that was not necessary.

Mike asked Jamal if he had scored any action yet and he said "No, not yet. But I'm going to get some before I call it a night". Mike gave Jamal the short version of how Trish's first had gone that night and told him he hadn't seen her for a while and that she was probably having her second (or second AND third) as we spoke.

Jamal showed his interest to Mike about Trish, asking general questions like height, weight, boob size. Mike answered his questions and Jamal responded saying, "Yeah, I'd like some of that!"

"Cool" Mike said, without feeling any need to take it any further than that.

It was about that time that Trish appeared at the door to the party room. She was alone and looking for Mike. Once she saw him, she stepped inside the suite and headed his way.

Mike asked her "Where you been?" and she answered, "Oh, I was with Herbert. You remember him; we met him at the last party. He wanted me to come down to his room for a while."

"Ah, ok." Was all Mike said. He wanted more details but he knew most of what there was to tell already. Mike did like the fact that this was someone Trish had fucked before. It allowed him to latch onto a quick visual that he knew would be a pretty accurate representation of what had just happened.

Mike introduced Trish to Jamal, whose eyes were definitely looking her up and down. Trish smiled and extended her hand to him as Mike simply came out and informed her, "Jamal said he really wants to get down with you."

"Oh really?" replied Trish, her eyes landing on Jamal much harder than she had done up until then. "Ok" was all she said and the three of them arose and headed down the hallway to Mike and Trisha's room. Mike knew Trisha very well. If someone wanted her, that usually made her want him.

This time, Trish was not interested in engaging in a lot of fore play. She jump started things by setting on the side of the bed and pulling Jamal's belt towards her. She un-did it quickly and reached in and grabbed his dick and immediately began sucking him off.

Once she was satisfied that it was firm enough, she pushed him down on the bed and pulled off the swim top and cast it away. As Mike had suspected, the swim top was the only article of clothing she was wearing at this point of the night.

He chuckled to himself when he thought of the closet and drawers filled with a dozen different ensembles that Trish had wanted available to her that night. At least she could just re-pack all of them for next time. She would not have to wash them either.

As soon as Trish mounted Jamal, she reached down to guide his dick into her. He was very well endowed, nearly ten inches and thick, as they say. Trish seemed to have no trouble guiding it into her. She humped the shit out of Jamal until her legs just started to give out on her and she rolled off and he got on top of her. Mike could hear the slap sounds as each of their pelvic areas connected, and he heard lots of gushy sounds.

"Cum left over from Herbert no doubt," Mike thought. He must have really filled her up. Jamal did not seem to mind the mess at all. In fact, due to his size, he probably welcomed the extra lubrication.

About this time, Mike saw that a couple of new men were standing at the doorway watching the action. Mike motioned them to come in if they wanted to. With big smiles on their faces, they came in and started watching. One of them set on the empty bed while the other one leaned against the dresser. They did as they should without being told and kept quite except for a couple of comments one of them made to Mike about how hot Trish looked.

"Man, I gotta have me some of that" the man said. Mike learned later on that these two guys were John and Phillip but he lost track about which one was John and which one was Phillip almost from the moment he heard the names.

Mike nodded slightly at the man's comment, although he wasn't telling the man (it was Phillip by the way) that he could have her. He was just agreeing that Phil SHOULD have her.

Mike knew that by now, Trish was probably getting to her limit. She tried to avoid overdoing things at these parties. He knew that she would be sore afterwards. Jamal was her third for the night and he was still hard at it. Mike had seen how Trish was wearing herself out on him when they first started fucking.

Jamal let everyone in the room know when he was climaxing in her. It was quite animated at it. Lots of "Oh baby, oh baby" comments. Mike could see that by the time Jamal finished, Trish was ready for him to be finished. I don't think Jamal even noticed that John and Phillip had come in to watch. He seemed to jump a bit when he turned and saw everyone watching him.

He made his exit pretty quickly, with limited conversation to any of us. He did stop and plant a kiss onto Trish's sweaty belly telling her "Later, baby", and left the room.

Trish just lay there, almost in a stupor. She was pretty much done in by then. Mike felt that she could care less that there was an audience, looking at her naked body as she caught her breath. Mike guessed that John and Philip were waiting to see what would happen next. Would she just continue to lay there naked in front of them or would she get up and go pee.

No one was speaking and then, almost like it had been rehearsed, both John and Phillip climbed into the bed beside her, one on each side. When they saw that she wasn't objecting, they started kicking off their shoes and pulling at the rest of their clothes and tossing them on the floor.

Mike thought that it was more a case of her not even realizing these two new dudes were there. She was just too worn out and exhausted. Mike wondered whether he should put a stop to it and was just about to suggest, "Maybe the lady is a bit too tired right now" when Philip spoke to her gently.

"Hi sweetie, my goodness you look good." John let her know he was there also by speaking to her. Mike had been right about one thing, Trish was not aware that two new guys had climbed into bed with her. She thought it was still Jamal with her.

She was spent but her exhaustion had the effect of mellowing her out, making her extremely passive. She spoke to them both "Well, hello. Where did you guys come from?"

"We came here to meet you, honey" Phillip told her, and put emphasis on the word YOU as he said it.

"Oh?" Trish replied. Very submissively Mike thought.

This was all the two guys needed as a green light and they both snuggled in closer to her and began exploring her body with their hands. Mike noticed that Trish had extended her arm and had grasped John's extremely hard dick with her hand and was squeezing and releasing it, squeezing and releasing. At this point, Mike leaned back and said to himself, "She's ok." Nevertheless, he worried about whether she could handle both of these people.

The foreplay didn't last very long, John mounted her first and in less than five minutes, he put another load up into her soaked coochie. Mike did the math and realized that John was her fourth for the night and she probably had three men's cum inside her now. He wasn't sure if her private session with Herbert had been cleaned up but he didn't think so.

As soon as john finished using her, he had no interest in hanging around to talk about it and just got dressed and left the room without a word to anyone. Mike was sure that if Trish had been more aware of her surroundings, that she probably would not have been that interested in John.

John had been really vocal with her while he was fucking her. Lots of what Mike and Trish codenamed "pillow talk". It is when there is a significant reference to racial aspects. Terms like *Big Black Dick* and *White Pussy* exchanged between Trish and her partner. When a man did it right and made her comfortable that the word play was part of the *play*, and not meant offensively, Trish was up for significantly more intense talk where words such as bitch, whore, cunt, etc was used.

Trish did draw the line with the N-word, even if the guy wanted it in the exchanges. John never asked her if he could verbally go after her and Mike was glad that Trish probably did not take notice of the names he applied to her during the act.

Mike did have a real passion for hearing a man get really down and dirty with the language. He had a few guys who hit him up on Yahoo Instant Messaging that didn't think twice about hailing him with phrases like "How's that whore wife of yours tonight?" However, those guys would never get past Mike to actually meet Trisha.

Philip didn't waste any time getting himself ready to do her as John was gathering his clothes and putting them on as he hoped on one leg, then the other to put on his pants and head to the door.

"Bastard" Mike thought to himself as he watch John leaving. Then he turned his attention back towards the bed and now that it was just Phillip there, Mike saw that Phillip was gigantically endowed. Possibly the biggest dick he had ever seen, something over twelve inches and a massive circumference. Mike worried about Trish being able to accommodate it.

Philip was well aware of his size. Many times, he had done the hard work of seducing a woman only to have her back out in fear of his mighty meat. He did not want this to be another one of those times. He looked over at Mike and saw the fear Mike had but Philip just nodded and somehow, let Mike know that he would take it easy with her and be willing to back off if she couldn't take it.

Trisha had not seen it. She had not even felt it yet other than some brushes her body had made against it while John had fucked her. She was exhausted and knew she should call it a night but she felt that she could handle one more... as long as it was quick like that other jerk had been. So she simply allowed him to mount her and to begin penetrating her.

At first, she was ok with it and then she began to feel stretched out by its width and she recoiled from it slightly. Philip felt her backing away from it and he stopped pushing towards her and as slowly as he could, fucked her with just the part of himself that had been successfully inserted so far. This still was larger around than Trish was accustomed to but she was as loose inside as she possibly could be. Philip continued to slide it in and out of her; she started to feel things that were good and not painful.

"That's nice," she murmured to Philip. "You are really BIG!" she added.

"I know baby, I'll take it slow with you, ok?" Philip whispered.

Mike could hear the exchange, and felt it was OK to let things continue but he was really watching closely. This was not about seeing Trish being fucked right now. This was something different. Philip was helping Trish to overcome his size. It was almost like a physical therapist assisting someone to take those first steps after suffering a broken leg.

Trish was doing fine with things too. Mike could see that she was definitely enjoying it now. That this very slow and deliberate in and out action was feeling good to her. He also noticed that Philip was getting deeper and deeper inside his wife. Trish was making more and more moans of pleasure and finally, Mike saw that Philip had buried himself inside her, in her all the way.

The pelvic movements Philip was making were still really slow and gentle although he had picked up the pace a bit and Trish seemed to be getting more and more into it. Mike realized that Trish has been overcome by the physical side of what was happening. The room could spin and she would not realize it. He saw her reaching levels of pleasure that he had never seen her obtain before. Not with anyone. By the time it was over, Philip was hitting her at full speed and Mike felt that Trish was receiving the best fuck of her life. She was too.

As it ended, Mike had several thoughts rush into his head. One was, that he did not think Trish was finished. He wasn't sure WHERE she was at right now, but she was taking this, taking to it like nothing he had ever seen before. His second thought was that Philip probably came like a garden hose in her.

Big hung men like Philip usual produced enormous amounts of semen. Lastly, he felt gratitude towards Philip. Philip had done this with the precision of a watchmaker. Never pushing her over the edge but keeping her on the edge for the entire encounter. She had loved it and Mike was thrilled for her.

After a few moments, Philip slid off her but he had left his giant dick inside her, throbbing in her for quite a while first. Just the vibrations emanating from this man's dick after he came was doing 'good stuff' for Trish.

As he pulled out of her, Trisha gasped yet again. She felt so empty at that moment, it took her breath away. However, this also allowed her to relax her body, for the first time in at least half an hour and the release she felt zapped everything she had left away and she closed her eyes and instantly fell asleep.

Philip looked towards Mike, smiled, and whispered. "Do you think she would mind if I stayed with her tonight? Is that ok with you too?"

"Yeah," Mike whispered back. "You are more than welcome to stay" and after another few seconds, Mike arose from the chair he had been setting in for a long time now and started getting undressed. He pulled down the sheets of his bed, walked towards the room door to close it, pausing by the bathroom on his way back to pee. When he finished, he turned off the bathroom light, which had been the only light illuminating the room.

Mike and Phillip continued to chat for a few more moments there in the dark before they both decided to call it a night. Mike learned that Philip was a divorced man that lived less than fifteen miles away from where he and Trish lived.

Both men joined Trisha in sleep-land quickly then. However, the sounds of moans coming from the other bed a couple of hours later were loud enough to wake up Mike. Although there were no lights on, there was enough light coming from streetlights outside the room and Mike saw that Philip was at her once more. He just smiled to himself and rolled over and went back to sleep.

In the months that followed, Trish and Mike saw a lot of Philip. He was often a weekend guest although Trish occasionally spent the weekend at Philips place. There had even been some chats about the possibility of Philip moving in with Trish and Mike but nothing definite yet. It would happen however, about six months later.

The three of them went out for breakfast the next morning. Trisha actually had difficulty walking. She had no strength in her legs and both Mike and Philip had to assist her. Philip followed Mike and Trisha home but just so they could show him where they lived. He did not stay, just long enough to wave goodbye but Trisha made sure he got a nice kiss before he left.

It was a week before Trish felt she was up to play again. Philip was every bit as gentle as he had been the first time. Yet Trish was not able to accommodate him. He was just too big. But this didn't stop them from trying. Philip visited again a couple of days later and another attempt was made but still, he was not able to completely penetrate her. However, they were able to complete a fuck. She was able to accept just enough of Philip so that he was able to get his nut. Using her mouth was out of the question of course.

But this had become a goal for everyone involved and on the next attempt, Phillip was able to bury himself into her again although it was a struggle and somewhat painful for Trish. But slowly, she found that she was able to handle the big man. They had to use a lot of KY Jelly for a while but over time, this became unnecessary.

One day a couple of months later, the three of them were out on the back deck having a BBQ. Mike almost choked on his hot dog when Philip wisecracked that he was going to start working on Trish's ass next. She did not think that was the least bit funny.

One unfortunate side effect of all this was that Trish no longer felt satisfied with the guys at the black on white parties. She just didn't get the feeling she had become accustomed to and Mike was a little bitter about this, he had enjoyed those parties in his own way every bit as much as Trish did in hers.

Her lack of, well, fulfillment, at the parties took away a lot of Mike's fun as well. Worse, his own sex with Trisha pretty much went down the toilet. She had changed down there, she had been remodeled, and it was like a pencil trying to fuck a donut for them now.

However, Phillip was more than adequate to supply what Trish had to have now. He was very happy as well. It had been his size and sexual appetites that had caused his first wife to walk out on him. He liked being a single man and his relationship with Mike and Trish was just perfect. He rarely attempted sex with anyone except Trish now and he was quite content with that.

William, the dude who continued to host parties in Charlotte, was sorry that he had not gotten around to banging Trisha at least once, but even more, he regretted losing one of his best white bitches.

Other works by I. M. Telling

Novels:

The Ebony Letter

The Ebony Letter is a tale of two couples who will never meet face to face nor exchange emails or connect on FaceBook. The story is presented from the perspective of each of the husbands. One man, The Reader, will discover the world that The Writer has lived in for many years.

The Reader is seduced by what he reads, and enters into a world of fantasy and envy. He is both repulsed and attracted by what The Writer has recorded within a journal. A journal once lost and now found.

This is the story of how The Reader is trapped by his own fantasies. He is unaware of how he is being changed and is slowly led towards an ultimate climax that he never expected nor thought he truly wanted.

Some fantasies are best left as fantasies.

http://www.amazon.com/dp/B007PYHBQA

Printed in Great Britain
by Amazon.co.uk, Ltd.,
Marston Gate.